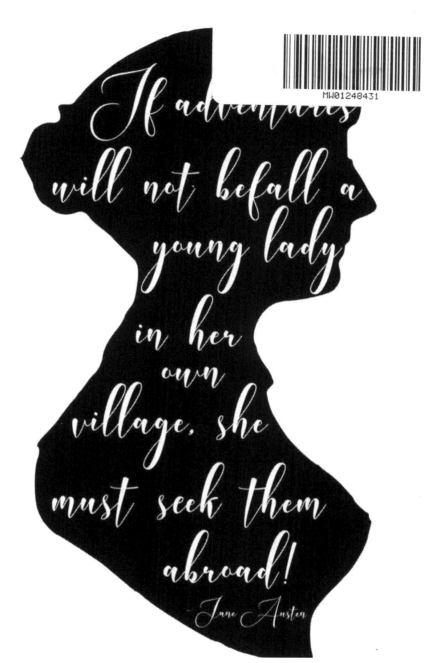

If adventures will not befall a young lady in her own village, she must seek them abroad!

Jane Austen

This Book Belongs To

_____

HABIT/GOAL TRACKER

Start Date:

Habit/Goal	1	2	3	4	5	6	7	8	9	10	11	12	13	14	15	16	17	18	19	20	21	22	23	24	25

If adventures will not befall a young lady in her own village, she must seek them abroad!

— Jane Austen

Thank you for your support. We hope you enjoy your new notebook. As a token of our appreciation, below is an QR Code for you to download and enjoy a **free** Jane Austen quote 8x10 printable PDF*:

* For Personal Use Only

For more amazing journals and adult coloring books from Penelope Pewter, visit:
Amazon.com
CuteNotebooksandJournals.com
www.InspirationalWares.com

She Believed She Could
So She Did Adult Coloring Book
with Inspirational Quotes

The Be A Pineapple Adult
Coloring Book

YOGA
An Adult Coloring Book

The Adult Coloring Book for
Coffee Lovers

Made in the USA
Columbia, SC
05 February 2022

55351971R00059